This edition published by Parragon in 2014
Parragon
Chartist House
15-17 Trim Street
Bath BA1 1HA, UK
www.parragon.com

ISBN 978-1-4454-6630-9

Printed in China

Doctor Pig

Written by Emily Gale

Illustrated by Mark Marshall

PaRragon

Bath • New York • Cologne • Melbourne • Delhi
Hong Kong • Shenzhen • Singapore • Amsterdam

Finley Pig was happy.

"Ahhhh!"

Life couldn't be better.

"It's alright for some!" said Agatha Chicken who was always sticking her beak in. "This is a busy farm, Lazybones," she clucked.

"I'm not Lazybones,
I'm Finley."

"Cheeky pig!" Agatha flapped
her wings, and squawked until
Finley ran away.

Finley sat under a tree to think.
Mud baths were lovely, but he did want
to be a big help on the busy farm.
What would he be good at?

"I've got it!"

Mummy Pig was puzzled.
"Where are you going with all that, Finley?"

"It's not Finley,
it's Doctor Pig!
And I'm late for
my first patient."

"What seems to be the trouble, Mrs. Moo?"

Mrs. Moo moo'd.

"Don't say moo, say ahhh!" said Finley.

"Finley, there's nothing wrong with my leg."

"Hold still for
Doctor Pig,
please!"

Chester Sheep was not good
at having his heart
listened to – he wouldn't
stop munching.

munch munch

munch

The geese, Heidi and Dora,
refused their medicine.

The sheepdog . . .   ran away.

Being a doctor was really hard work, but the
most difficult patients of all were . . .

. . . the
chickens.

At the end of a long day, Mummy Pig
was pleased to see Finley.

"I'm very good at being a doctor," said Finley. "But I'm . . .

"...even better at being me.

Do Not Disturb

Ahhhh!"

Life couldn't be better.